He has always been interested in writing and decided to take his interest further by writing a book during lockdown from his job at a primary school.

Being a father and a grandfather, this had given him plenty of experiences that he has been able to work into his book.

Prior to working at a school as a Learning Support Assistant he trained as a design draughtsman working on domestic and industrial heating controls.

His main passion is sport, having played badminton and football at county level and table tennis at league level. He's a keen runner having completed three London marathons and 15 half marathons.

My wife, Norma, daughter, Julie, and sister, Pat.

Peter King

Outnumbered by Daughters

Austin Macauley Publishers™
LONDON • CAMBRIDGE • NEW YORK • SHARJAH

Copyright © Peter King 2023

The right of Peter King to be identified as author of this work has been asserted by the author in accordance with sections 77 and 78 of the Copyright, Designs and Patents Act 1988.

All rights reserved. No part of this publication may be reproduced, stored in a retrieval system, or transmitted in any form or by any means, electronic, mechanical, photocopying, recording, or otherwise, without the prior permission of the publishers.

Any person who commits any unauthorised act in relation to this publication may be liable to criminal prosecution and civil claims for damages.

This is a work of fiction. Names, characters, businesses, places, events, locales, and incidents are either the products of the author's imagination or used in a fictitious manner. Any resemblance to actual persons, living or dead, or actual events is purely coincidental.

A CIP catalogue record for this title is available from the British Library.

ISBN 9781398474444 (Paperback)
ISBN 9781398474451 (ePub e-book)

www.austinmacauley.com

First Published 2023
Austin Macauley Publishers Ltd ®
1 Canada Square
Canary Wharf
London
E14 5AA

Chapter 1
A Time to Reflect on the Past

Weekends are a busy time, especially on a Saturday morning and I wouldn't have it any other way. The bungalow has long since been the central meeting place for all of Ella's friends. We never know who is going to drop in. Having also done the weekly shop my priority now is the garden. Sitting on my own with a well-deserved cup of tea I was able to catch my breath for the first time in ages and let my mind wander and reflect on how far this family has come. Life was full on but with a family of three young girls, I guess I shouldn't expect anything different. Ella at the age of nearly twelve was now capable of stroppy mood swings and was always pushing boundaries. She was winning her fair share of arguments with me at the age of three so what chance did I have now. Rosie and Zoe being three years younger still had stable personalities but at times could be influenced by Ella.

My previous dabble at romance with Meg and Sue had not finished well for one reason and another, so that side of my life had been shelved indefinitely. But that said, I did look forward to my jogging sessions with Sarah and her helping me out at Spartan's training sessions.

On reflection, Meg and Sue were always going to be part of our lives. So much has happened in the past for us all for them not to be, but only as good friends. Meg and I were still active members of the local Friday night badminton club and would always go together, with Mia sleeping over as it was usually a late night and Meg didn't want to leave her on her own in the flat. Their daughters Mia and Maisie are very special to me and both were very close to becoming my stepdaughter at one time. I've known Maisie since Reception and have shared so many memories with her, some good and some not so good. Taking her to meet her father after an absence of eight years was very traumatic. Looking after her while her mum was in the hospital and reluctantly coming to me for help while she was self-harming were particularly stressful times for her. I thought about the time when I made a promise to look after Mia permanently if her mum didn't recover from a very serious illness. That was touch and go for a long time and very worrying for Mia who stayed with us for a long time before moving back home.

Thinking about Meg and Sue and now finally knowing the reason why they cannot bare to be in the same room as each other, despite my previous attempts to do so. Sue is never going to forgive Meg for having an affair with her partner, with Mia being a product of that relationship. Their unfriendliness has impacted Mia and Maisie's friendship as they felt they had to be loyal to their mums. Hopefully, this will all change when they finally learn that they are half-sisters. They are so different and sadly have nothing in common.

I then turned my thoughts to Ella. She is now beginning to be someone I don't particularly like on occasions. How could I ever think that of my own step-daughter? I feel so wicked when those thoughts come into my head. I was warned that I will be facing more difficult times ahead as the girls grow up. By my reckoning, I am there now with Ella. She now has a cold and hurtful side to her and when things don't go her way she is happy to remind me that I'm not her real dad and don't have a say in any matters concerning her. She can be so unkind to Rosie and Zoe and quite often reduces Rosie to tears. If the mood takes her she shuts herself in her room without a goodnight or anything and usually, the frostiness continues the next morning. Meg and Sue are experiencing something similar with their daughters so I'm not alone. At least I will be prepared for it when Rosie and Zoe become older. They seem really settled now, with Rosie no longer asking me to find her a mum. I thought I had now come a long way in understanding girls' needs, what with trainer bras, periods and personality changes as 'hormones' kick in. I certainly will be more prepared when Rosie and Zoe reach that stage. Besides I'm sure Ella will put me right if I get it wrong. Why are young girls so complicated?

I remembered that today is the anniversary of my first wife's passing which understandably brought a tear to my eyes. I conceded that although the girls brought me a great deal of happiness I still had bouts of loneliness from time to time and have bitter thoughts as to how life has dealt me some cruel cards. At the age of thirty-four I've already lost two wives who I loved dearly, what other cards will life deal me I wondered? I was suddenly confronted by three girls dancing around me demanding tea. As it was Saturday and they stay up later I was in no hurry to vacate my chair until Rosie decided to jump on me.

"Dad, you have tears in your eyes, are you sad? Have we been naughty?" Spoken by a girl who doesn't have a naughty bone in her body.

"I've got some grit in my eyes, it's become very windy." I could see Ella giving me a knowing look, very little gets past her.

That evening as I tucked Ella in and was about to say goodnight, she grabbed my hand. "Dad can we talk? Come and sit down on the side of the bed."

"This sounds serious," I remarked. "Were you reminiscing about your very sad past? Was that why you were upset when we came to find you?"

"Yes, today is the anniversary of my first wife's passing."

"Please tell me about her."

"She was very sick and she knew that but she had one wish and that was to get married. Everyone was so kind and helpful and two weeks later we were married. Unfortunately, she was too weak for us to have a honeymoon and the marriage lasted just two weeks." By this time we both had tears in our eyes. "I was also thinking about your mum and you not getting to meet your real dad."

"You are my real dad don't you know, he is just a photo." "Mum never spoke much about him and never told me how he died."

"I think she wanted to wait until you were older. He died in a motorbike accident and sadly didn't know that your mum was expecting you. He would have been so proud of you."

"I keep his photo under my pillow."

"I know you do."

"How do you know that?"

"I always remake your bed after you have just thrown the covers over."

"Do you mind it being there?"

"Of course not, if it gives you comfort."

"Dad I love you so much you are so understanding."

"Ella let's finish this conversation on a happy note before we go to bed. How far does your memory take you back?"

"I remember you teaching me how to kick a ball as I was always falling over trying, you buying my first ball, you always making bath time fun and taking me swimming." "You weren't even three years old then. You have a very good memory. I can remember when your mum and your nan first came round to the bungalow, you were very tired so I laid you down on my bed for a sleep. I stayed with you in case you rolled off the bed and I thought then you were the love of my life and nothing has changed."

"I do remember because I wet your bed. Dad, we are so close, please don't let it ever change, even if I have horrible moments."

"It won't." With that, I tucked Ella in, a big hug and a kiss on the forehead and went contented to my bedroom.

Chapter 2
Keeping Family Time a Priority

After tea on a Saturday, I try so hard to organise a board game so that we are doing something together. Apart from meal times, it is one of the only times we sit down as a family. With three reluctant girls, the game never lasts long. I have long since thought that the girls sit there going through the motions of playing just to please me. I do not look forward to bath times. It is chaotic but it shouldn't be with two bathrooms. Rosie and Zoe no longer share a bath and argue every night as to who is going first, despite a rota being in place. With Zoe being the stronger personality Rosie always ends up in tears. As Ella is now becoming a very private person as far as her growing body is concerned the bathroom is now strictly out of bounds when she has a bath. Recently I was never comfortable being asked to wash her hair or sit in the corner for a chat, so I am pleased about that. Before I get down to some serious marking which seems always endless, I have to remind myself to split my time with their bedtime routine equally between them as they have different ways of relaxing before lights out. Rosie always likes a bedtime story and a big hug. One is never enough for her and I always get called back for another. Zoe thinks she is too old for a story so we usually do some colouring. I am really honoured that she now trusts me to colour between the lines as she is a perfectionist. A kiss on the forehead and a hug are more than enough for her and I know it is really for my benefit. Ella, once she is out of the bathroom, sits down with me with a hot drink and a chat as she is much older. Tonight with a very important league game tomorrow for Spartans she is keen to voice her opinion on who should be the subs. Her routine is a kiss and a hug and a blown kiss as I go out the door. These adorable routines set me up for an hour of marking before I go to bed.

I awoke early Sunday morning awaiting my usual Sunday morning visit from Zoe, asking why she has to go to watch football when she hates it. Zoe was the odd one out as she disliked any form of sport. Ella was an exceptional footballer and Rosie was showing great promise, although younger than any other of the girls in the team, good enough to come on as a sub in Spartan's matches. True to form Zoe arrived first and promptly got under the covers. "Dad I know I have got to go to football but can I take something to do while we are there?"

"Of course, you can, what did you have in mind."

"My big colour by numbers picture I got for Christmas and would you help me colour it after I've done my homework, please? I need a piggy promise from you in case you forget."

"I won't forget," I replied and with that, she was gone. Rosie appeared next looking very sleepy. All she wanted to do was to snuggle in bed. Ella has now gone from being the first up to the last and has to be coaxed out of bed even on match days.

On arrival Sarah was already there, warming up the girls when I was approached by some of the parents who were curious about the system the girls play and how it works so that they could understand what is going on during the game. "I might have to get you all to sign the official secrets act before I tell you," I jokingly replied. Fortunately, I had a whiteboard with me which made it easier to follow with diagrams. I explained that I first tried the line formation system out with Year 6 at school, during league and cup matches last season for both girls and boys teams. It certainly confuses the opposition, especially if they try to mark players. You will notice that our wingers will switch a couple of times during the game and although we don't go into marking specific players if the opposition does have an outstanding player, Charlotte who plays just in front of the keeper will follow her all the time she is in our half, with Amelia then covering her position. The two wingers have the most to do because they have to either be a wing defender or a wing attacker depending on where the ball is. As they cover the most ground during the game they are the ones that usually come off during the second half. "Are all the girls comfortable with the system?" one dad asked.

"Absolutely, six of the girls that are in the team played in the successful Year 6 team at school and the four newcomers took to it straight away." With that, I joined the team for a team talk.

Being in a higher division the matches aren't so friendly and some of the tacklings are 'X' rated. This match was no exception causing me to have a word with the referee at halftime about calming it down. A 2-0 win and I was pleased for it to end without any of the team getting seriously hurt.

While I was talking to the other coach I was aware of a man talking to Alexa. I immediately approached him and asked if I could help. I soon realised it was a coach from another club trying to persuade her to join his club. I showed my annoyance by saying it would have been courteous to have asked my permission before talking to Alexa, which is against the rules and I will be putting in a complaint with the league. Now poaching goes on all the time and although Alexa is registered to play for Spartans, she could easily cancel it and join another club if she so wished. She is an outstanding striker who scores goals for fun and I know she has been watched by other clubs. When I had calmed down I took the other coach's email address and said that I would talk to her and if she is interested I would let him know, as it is her choice. Although no way did I want to lose her.

Sunday afternoon is traditionally homework time. They were good girls in that respect and just got down to it. I called it homework club because it wasn't unusual for Alexa, Maisie, or Mia to turn up on the doorstep and join them if they had problems understanding what they had to do. Especially Maisie who was struggling in a lower maths group at her school. Rosie was similar. I would take the opportunity to try and mark some class books but usually, I'm on hand to help out with any problems. The girls always stay for tea before their mums pick them up. The mums were always grateful because it was a good way to get the homework done without stress.

Later that afternoon I answered the door to Sarah and Alexa. "Are you here for homework club Alexa?"

"No we actually wanted to talk to you about Spartans," replied Alexa.

"I'm sorry you were put in an awkward position by that coach. He was out of order talking to you. He should have asked permission and only spoken to you with either your mum or me with you. That said you should know that several coaches have shown an interest in you, but this is the first time a coach has tried to poach you. That is because you are a very good striker and have a nose for scoring goals and getting better every game. You are currently registered to play for Spartans and no other team. But if you are unhappy and feel you can do better playing for another team, I wouldn't stand in your way and would cancel your registration. What are your thoughts Alexa, did you want to have more time and have a further talk with your mum?"

"No, I would very much like to carry on playing for Spartans please."

"I'm so pleased Alexa, thank you, no way did I want to lose you. Sarah shall we have a cup of tea to celebrate?"

After they had gone I was thinking about Sarah. I knew so little about her, mind you I hadn't told her about my complicated past either. My relationship with her was uncomplicated. If I can ever call it a relationship. Is there a husband or boyfriend in her life, who knows? At Spartans and parents evening she has always been on her own. When we are jogging together we usually talk about our schools or football.

Chapter 3
The Birthday Weekend

As we were getting ready for school the following morning I mentioned to Ella that she needs to think about her birthday and whether she is too old to have a party. "Dad I'm never too old for a party how can you ever think that," came her very indignant reply.

"Ella, I'm teasing you, of course, you should have a party. Give it some thought and we can talk about it tonight."

"I don't need to think about it. I would like to have a mini sports tournament as in previous years. You always organise a smashing party for me. I do have a problem though, which friends to invite."

"Well, how many were you thinking?"

"I will make a list tonight."

"Daddy can we invite a friend as well because we won't know anybody," asked Rosie.

"You had better ask Ella it's her party." The girls can always find something to distract them from getting ready so I cannot relax until we are all seat belted in the car. Having parked the car at school, Ella walks the short distance to her school while the twins head for the school's morning club. I then go to my classroom to prepare for the morning lessons.

Monday after school I run a school football club. Rosie takes part and Ella comes and helps me while Zoe goes to an after-school art club. So the arrangement works well.

That evening after her bath, as arranged we talked about her party. She had a list of sixteen girls she wanted to invite, so holding it in the garden was not an option. I decided to look into the possibility of hiring a sports hall, either at the badminton club or at school. Ella wanted to play badminton, football and netball and have competitions as previous parties. All sixteen girls said yes to coming and I was amazed at the number of mums who wanted to help me with the food. We couldn't agree on Maisie. Ella didn't want to invite her as she hated all forms of sport. But I said she could help me with the scoreboard as she did last year, so that was settled without too much argument.

I phoned Sue to tell her about Ella's party arrangements hoping that she would come but knowing that she wouldn't if Meg was there. I wanted to speak to Maisie and ask her if she could help me with the running of the competitions and with the scoreboard as she did last year but she wouldn't come out of her room to speak to me. Sue said that as soon as she comes home from school she spends most of her time crying in her room. I asked whether she was self-harming again but Sue didn't know as she hardly ever speaks to her. Sue asked if I could spend some time with her and find out what is really worrying her. So it was agreed that Sue would bring Maisie on Saturday. She would keep an eye on the girls while Maisie and I went for a walk.

Saturday morning and a very tearful Maisie arrived with her mum. After walking in silence which seemed like an age,

I opened the conversation. "Maisie, I am so worried about you. You are very special to me and always will be."

With that Maisie began to cry. "Please give me a hug I am so sad." We were now so close to the local café and as Maisie hadn't had any breakfast we decided to carry on with our conversation afterwards. Having breakfast and a hot drink Maisie cheered up.

"Maisie, please tell me why you are so sad, I'm sure talking about it would help."

"I wish we could do this more often, as I feel so lonely."

"Maisie, I'm only a phone call or a text message away and you can always visit. I have to ask you whether you have been self-harming again." The long pause suggested to me that she had. She reluctantly showed me her arms and talked about feeling worthless, having no friends, or any love in her life and she is struggling with her lessons at school. I sat there listening to her saying that she is not very close to her mum at the moment. She couldn't help her or cope with her because she has problems of her own and is just as unhappy and depressed as she was. She mentioned that I was the only one she could turn to and she felt closer to me than anyone. I then asked her what needed to be done to change all this and make her happy. She said by saying that she wanted to be part of my family, which she thought she was going to be.

We were back at the bungalow in no time at all, having persuaded her to come to Ella's party and help me. Retelling my conversation with Maisie to Sue was very emotional as she was in tears before I had even started. But she had to be told exactly what was said. Thinking back to her primary school days Maisie had several bouts of depression then. Eventually opening up and talking about feeling worthless, having no friends, being unloved and feeling isolated. So nothing has changed. Sue blamed herself as she was so preoccupied with her feelings and problems she hadn't noticed how bad Maisie was.

On the day of Ella's party, she was the first one up, padding into my bedroom. It was just like old times with Ella with only her face showing above the bed covers. As with previous parties, she was mainly worried about whether all her friends would turn up. It wasn't long before Rosie and Zoe appeared, fighting for their usual positions in my bed.

As the party was due to start at two o'clock we decided to spend some time at the school in the morning setting it all up. Before we knew it, it was party time, although not soon enough for Ella. All the girls turned up in sports gear as planned. All the mums stayed to help with the tea organised by Meg. All I had to do was supply the birthday cake. As there was no sign of Maisie. Zoe helped me with the scoring and keeping the scoreboard up to date. I had arranged medals for all the girls and a small indoor plant for all the mums, with Zoe doing the presentation. As all the girls and mums knew each other and got on so well the party didn't finish very early as there was no time limit. When we had cleared up and arrived home it was too late for baths, so a clean of teeth and a quick wash and then to bed.

In no time at all it was lights out but not before Ella called me back into her bedroom and promptly burst into tears. "Dad you give me so much unconditional love regardless of how I behave to you. I feel so ashamed about my behaviour and the things I say to you. Especially about you not being my real dad. I'm so sorry and you do know that I never mean what I say when I say horrible things to you. I do love you so much."

"Look no one should be crying when they have just had their birthday party. Did you enjoy it?"

"It was smashing, it gets better every year."

"I can't pretend that it doesn't hurt when you throw it in my face that I'm not your real dad especially as we have been through so much together in the past. So I do hope you never mean it."

"Please give me a big hug and tell me I'm forgiven."

"Time to sleep now you have a big day ahead of you tomorrow, your birthday. Ella was very pleased with her surprise birthday presents and as there wasn't a match that morning we decided to go out to lunch at a place of her choice. As it was a lovely afternoon Ella asked if we could all go out for a bike ride to the local park. Back to reality when we arrived back with homework club. But as no other members arrived, all the homework was finished in time to watch a video before bedtime routine. No complaints there for once as the girls were very tired from their late night at the party.

Chapter 4
The Truth Finally Comes Out

I text Maisie to find out why she didn't come to Ella's party, but as I didn't have the usual immediate reply I then phoned Sue, again no reply and I then became worried. Not that I could do anything with the girls asleep. As Maisie went to a different school than Ella, I had no way of knowing whether she had been going to school.

That evening as I was in the middle of marking Sue finally returned my many calls. She was so upset and took a while to tell me that Maisie was back in hospital again, seriously ill with a blood infection caused by a deep cut on her stomach. She had been self-harming yet again but this time taking it much further. Sue admitted that she has failed Maisie because she was so caught up with her own problems. I suggested that isn't it time to let Maisie and Mia know that they are half-sisters. That would surely lift Maisie's spirits and you would have Meg wanting to help. Sue was adamant that she and Meg would never be friends and wouldn't want her help even if she offered and now is not the time to tell Maisie about her half-sister. I reluctantly warned Sue that if her 'ex-partner ever finds out about Maisie's self-harming he might try for temporary custody. With that Sue asked whether Maisie could stay with us during the Easter holidays so that she could really sort herself out. I remarked that Easter would have been fine except I'm taking the girls on holiday to their favourite holiday camp for a few days. I followed that by saying that we could have her stay after that if it helps. I had to remind her how many times Maisie has stayed with us in the past, but nothing changed. Sue then remarked that all she wants is to be part of my family and she hadn't forgiven her for backing out of our relationship when she thought she was going to be my stepdaughter. Something she regretted so much. Sue in desperation then asked whether she could come with us if she was well enough. I sensed that Sue thought I was making excuses when I said that I hadn't managed to get a decent size chalet as I had only just booked on the spur of the moment. I felt so sorry for Sue when she reminded me that Maisie hates staying in the flat on her own while she works in case her dad turns up. I then asked whether there was any way she could take some time off and take Maisie away for a few days and get their relationship back on track. She pointed out that she has to work all hours that she can as she is behind with her rent. Having been so surprised to hear that I did ask whether her 'ex-partner is still paying maintenance as the courts had ruled. Having been told no I enquired whether her sister could help? That was a no too, as they didn't get on and hadn't spoken for some time. As Sue left I asked her to let me know if she wanted Maisie to stay when we come back.

Unfortunately, Ella had heard my conversation with Sue. "So Maisie and Mia are half-sisters and you are taking us on holiday at Easter. Please can we go on our own? I only want to share you with Rosie and Zoe." I knew that was coming. I remember when Sue and I were planning to get married. Ella hated the thought of Maisie becoming my stepdaughter and threw a massive tantrum.

"If she stays with us I won't talk to her and I won't let her share my bed."

"Where has your nice side gone?"

"It doesn't exist with Maisie. So that horrible man we saw in the park is Mia's dad as well."

"Ella, you must never say anything as Maisie and Mia don't know yet that they are half-sisters."

One evening we decided to visit Maisie in hospital with a reluctant Ella tagging along. I was shocked to find Maisie so unwell and only Sue could see her and only for a few minutes. Ella has always said that Maisie is attention seeking and that is why she self-harms. But I see a deeply unhappy girl who gets no enjoyment in life whatsoever. The nightly phone calls to Sue for an update have been less than encouraging with Sepsis now being considered. She had now changed her mind about telling Maisie that Mia is her half-sister, thinking that it just might cheer her up and give her something to focus on. Sue then asked a big favour. She wanted me to arrange a meeting with Meg and herself and the two girls, not at her flat but at my bungalow, to try and mend their friendship and tell the girls together, once Maisie was out of the hospital. I said that it had nothing to do with me and I should not be involved, but Sue felt she wouldn't be able to do it on her own, so reluctantly I agreed to be a spokesperson on such a delicate matter.

Two weeks later Maisie was finally discharged from the hospital. Maisie and Mia looked stunned to see both their mums in the same room together. Having told the girls that they were half-sisters, the girl's reaction certainly wasn't what the mums expected. Both girls burst into tears with Maisie rushing out of the room followed very closely by Sue also crying. Later when things were calmer Mia had the most concerns. She remembered she had seen Maisie's father when she was playing in the park with Ella and Maisie. She thought at the time that he was horrible but now she has found out that he is her father too. After a barrage of questions mainly from Mia, she was relieved to hear that he didn't know about her and wouldn't be trying to contact her in the near future. I asked the girls were they pleased to find out that they each had a half-sister now they have had time to think about it. Neither would answer but Mia did ask why they hadn't been told earlier. I told them that was a decision made by your mums.

As time past nothing had changed. The two mums were no friendlier, nor the two girls who just ignored each other.

Chapter 5
Two Departures from
Our Family Friendship Group

Taking the girls for a short holiday camp holiday at Easter was just what we needed. But it didn't sit easy with Sue who thought that we should have taken Maisie. I did agree that Maisie could stay with us for a few days afterwards, against Ella's wishes', but Sue didn't take up the offer. Which I felt was strange as Maisie hated staying in their flat while her mum worked. Despite that, we weren't ever short of company. Mia was a regular visitor and the twins who had previously complained that it wasn't fair that they never had any friends to come and play, both had their best friends to stay for tea. Alexa also stayed while Sarah and I went for a jog or played tennis a couple of mornings.

During one of our evening chats Ella remarked that it is clear that Sarah and me do like each other, why don't you admit it. I played that remark down by saying that romance is the last thing I want at this moment of time, with my track record of broken romances. Besides, it's not fair on you girls, secretly hoping you would get a step-mum and it all falling through. Ella pointed out that they don't need a mum as I do the job very well. Later with Ella in bed, I did wonder whether I should perhaps put more effort into my friendship with Sarah. I know she meets up with a teacher from her school from time to time, so she probably hasn't even considered me as romantic material anyway. I decided that next time I go jogging with Sarah I will try and bring up the subject. Two days later my big chance came. I was so nervous. It reminded me of when I went to see my girlfriend's dad to ask for my first wife's hand in marriage. It was planned that I would call round on an evening when everyone had gone to bingo including my girlfriend. Two hours later I was still sitting there but managed to get approval just before they all arrived home. Sarah asked, "You are very thoughtful this morning is everything OK?"

"I have a question to ask you, but I'm worried I might be disappointed with your answer. Look I'm just going to come out with it regardless. Is there a husband or boyfriend on the scene, are you romantically involved with anyone at the moment?"

"That is the last thing I expected you to ask," replied Sarah.

"I hope I haven't embarrassed you but I have been wanting to ask you for some time."

"Where is this leading to?" said Sarah with a mischievous grin on her face.

"Please help me out here, I'm floundering and about to sink."

"I've dropped so many hints recently and you haven't taken them up so I assumed there was no interest," remarked Sarah, this time with a more serious expression on her face. "I look forward to seeing you and when I don't I miss you. I didn't dare raise my hopes because if we ever were to get serious I have three girls for you to consider. A big ask!"

"Can I ask you a question now? Am I competing with Meg and Sue?"

"No, you are not competing with anyone. There has been some history in the past but nothing came of it." We decided to take a breather and sit on a park bench as it was difficult to have a serious conversation while we were jogging.

"Just to bring you up to speed with my complicated past. I have been married twice. My first wife, my childhood sweetheart, was seriously ill and her greatest wish was to get married. Sadly the marriage lasted two weeks. My second wife, mother to the twins and Ella, unfortunately died of breast cancer. The twins are mine but Ella is my adopted stepdaughter. My late wife was very concerned that her partner's family would want to lay claim to Ella if they knew of her existence, so to give her peace of mind I adopted her."

"I suppose it is my turn now," replied Sarah.

"Alexa isn't actually mine. She belongs to my sister who unfortunately died of a brain haemorrhage shortly after giving birth. As far as Alexa is concerned I'm her mum. My sister would never say who the father is. I know one day I will have to tell her about her real mum." With that, I cuddled Sarah and gave her a gentle kiss on her cheek.

"I've been waiting for you to do that for some time." We sat there in silence holding hands for ages, before walking back stopping every so often for a hug and a lingering kiss. We eventually arrived back into the real world with the girls pleading they were starving.

It was a relationship that was deemed to grow slowly, with us both working at different schools and both being single parents. Apart from phone calls during the week, it was the weekends when we saw a great deal of each other, but with very little time for romance. Saturday morning is always set aside for jogging while Alexa stays with the girls. Sarah and Alexa always stay for lunch as do any of the friends that might have dropped by. Usually, by late afternoon everyone has gone home, giving me the chance to catch up with some washing and ironing. I then see Sarah at Spartans in the morning and later because although Alexa is in my class she likes to be part of the Sunday afternoon homework club. While I'm sorting out homework problems Sarah will organise tea. Sarah and I talked about this and agreed that we would find a way. I suggested that once in a while I would use my child minder who only lives a couple of doors away. We could go out for a meal perhaps on a Saturday night with Alexa staying over.

The girls sensed that something was going on between us because one break time when I was on duty, Alexa asked if her mum and I were seeing each other. I told her that I really enjoy being with your mum and hope that she feels the same. I went on to say that I really do hope something eventually comes of it, but being single parents you girls are our priority at the moment.

Keeping in touch with both Sue and Maisie regularly by phone was the best I could manage. Maisie would occasionally cycle over on a Sunday afternoon if she had problems with her homework but always seemed so withdrawn and tearful. Talking to both of them it struck me that Sue was in a worse place than Maisie. Sadly it turned out to be the case. The situation with Maisie, a shortage of money and being threatened with eviction for falling well behind with the rent finally pushed her over the edge. As much as I wanted to help her and felt very guilty for not doing so, I had to think of the girls. Sue needed a period of calmness and solitude and virtually full-time care. Having Maisie stay wouldn't have been too much of a problem, apart from Ella. As she no longer considered her as one of her friends. Meg was the other option for Maisie but claimed that there was no room in her small flat to be able to help. I just could not see that working out anyway, as Mia has not come to terms yet having Maisie as a half-sister.

One Saturday morning we had surprise visitors. It was Sue and Maisie armed with cakes. Just like old times I thought. The twins were very pleased to see Maisie but Ella was not so. While we were on our own with our coffee Sue just blurted it out. "I still have feelings for you. I cannot fight them any longer. They are just not going away. My biggest regret was changing my mind at the last minute about you and me. I thought I was being unfair to you as being on my own for such a long time I was very set in my ways."

"Sue you will always have a place in my heart, but we have been down this road a couple of times, what would be different this time if we decided to try again? The twins in particular were so upset before, they took rejection badly because they thought you were going to be their mum. Maisie was also looking forward to our families joining together. As tempting as it is, I just cannot risk them being so hurt again. If I was on my own things might be different."

"What if we took things slowly?"

"I think we have both moved on. What would be nice if we saw you and Maisie more often, sometimes we don't see you for weeks."

"Maisie, having you back in her life again would solve her self-harming for sure."

"I don't think it's a good idea to restart our romance just to give Maisie stability. Besides we have an open house here. Maisie knows she is welcome anytime. You recall it wasn't such a long time ago when you decided to keep Maisie away because you felt she was getting too close to me."

"I did it to save you any embarrassment," was Sue's reply.

"Most girls and boys have crushes on their teachers, it is a passing phase and part of growing up and harmless. Any future romance has to come from the heart and although I care for Maisie dearly and don't like seeing her so upset and insecure, us getting together would be for all the wrong reasons."

As soon as Sue and Maisie left the three girls circled me. The girls knew exactly what my conversation with Sue was all about. "Do you miss not having a woman in your life? We don't miss not having a mum in our life at all. You do the mum and dad role brilliantly. We can give you all the love you need," remarked Ella. I followed that by saying that I do get lonely sometimes, especially when you are all in bed. I usually throw myself into marking books to try and fill the void. That remark prompted big cuddles all around.

It was sometime after Sue and Maisie had vacated their flat and moved into the sister's three-bedroom house thirty miles away that I found out. It was almost like part of the family had suddenly disappeared out of our lives without even a goodbye. Meg wasn't at all bothered but I was extremely hurt. Sue must have felt so alone with neither myself nor Meg able to help long term. I gave up in the end leaving messages for them both. Clearly, we were now completely out of their lives. But I was very worried about Maisie because she thrived on routine and a big change like moving to a new school would be very traumatic for her. Still, Sue didn't have to worry about money problems anymore.

A couple of weeks later I did receive a phone call from Maisie. After a long pause, I was just about to hang up when – "It's me I just wanted to hear your voice."

"Maisie, I've been so worried about you. Why did you leave without saying goodbye?"

"Mum thought it best as it would be less painful for us."

"How is your mum?"

"She is slowly improving and we are getting on much better."

"Maisie and how are you? I'm missing you badly. If I could have found a way for you and your mum to move in I would have done so. But mum needed full-time care. I could have looked after you, but you and your mum need to be living together and not apart. I will always care for you, a stepdaughter that got away." With that Maisie started to cry as she said she would always love me.

I seemed to be the only one who cared. Ella and the twins certainly didn't and neither did Meg and Mia. They were soon forgotten, but not by me. I promised Maisie that she could come and stay during the holidays. although I knew deep down that it was unlikely to happen. She did ask if I could text her regularly and I made her promise to text me if she had any problems or worries.

Chapter 6
Family Life Is Not All Perfect Harmony

There are times when my classroom is my only calming place, my solitude. I had virtually complete control in the classroom, but now and then very little at home. Some mornings I couldn't wait to get to school, how sad is that. The twins were growing up fast and were now wearing training bras. and faced with periods. Although I no longer had Sue to guide me through this complicated stage, I was fairly confident having been introduced to that stage with Ella. What I wasn't prepared for was the monthly battleground that took place. Tantrums, mood swings and tears. How I wish I had a partner to share these times. The girls were always sorry afterwards. My attitude towards them changes as well which didn't help matters. I disliked them and didn't want them around me. I kept telling myself that this happens in every household during this time. But that is only small comfort as with three girls it seems to be never-ending. Still, it could have been four girls had romance been kinder to me. Parents with boys only know half of it.

Once Ella decided to give me a chapter and verse on the subject and how the girls feel at this time, I think I'm more understanding and try to keep the peace and stamp out arguments. When they are in bed and asleep then the guilt steps in. Knowing that I am going to have to face this for a very long time, I decided the next time it all flairs up, I would defuse the screaming and the tantrums by taking the opportunity to distract them by getting them together to talk about our summer holidays. The talk went very well. Each girl took a piece of paper and wrote down their preference from three options. While the girls were deciding I made them a drink. That idea didn't work well as the three girls ticked different options. So I decided to take matters into my own hands by saying that I will book a surprise holiday for all of us.

"Will you tell us before we go?" enquired Rosie.

"No, I will tell you on the morning we go. But one question, do want a friend to come with us or do we go on our own?"

"Can we go on our own please?" pleaded the girls.

A couple of days later the three girls came to see me.

"Dad, we can't wait until the day we go on holiday, can you tell us now?"

"I tell you what I will do. When I receive confirmation that the holiday is booked and it will be no point in you hunting for the paperwork because it will be looked away in my briefcase. When it is ten weeks before we go I will give you one clue each week. Now how does that sound?" I marked the date of the holiday on the calendar and Ella marked ten weeks back. They were so excited when they received the first clue. I pointed out that it will be like a jigsaw puzzle and they will need to keep each clue. Having been asked by both Meg and Sarah if I had thought about the summer holidays yet and having told them our plans, I certainly didn't expect their response. They both thought it would be a lovely change and could they come to? I explained the game of clues to find out where we were going and they agreed to play along as well. By week six they were no nearer guessing the destination, so I decided to make the remaining clues slightly easier. By this time the girls knew that Alexa and Mia were coming too, but seemed OK with that. Besides, it was two extra trying to solve the clues.

The day of the holiday departure the five girls still hadn't worked out where we were going. So as we were all being driven to the airport I decided to go through the answers to all the clues one by one before clue ten told them all they wanted to know. The shrieks of delight told Meg, Sarah and myself we had made the right decision. The remainder of the journey was spent fielding so many questions about the airport, what country and what is there to do when we get there? It was so nice to see the girls very excited. It was a new experience for them, flying and being in a hot country. All the hotel rooms were conveniently near to each other The three girls shared a room with a double and a single bed connected to my room.

To say the holiday was fabulous was an understatement. All the girls got on very well and joined in the entertainment. Alexa, Ella, Mia and Rosie played football every day, while I went swimming with Zoe and joined an art club with her to try and divide my time equally between the girls. We all went for bike rides. The highlight for the girls was the nightly disco. Although it wasn't a holiday where romance could play a big part Meg sensed that Sarah and I were getting on really well and began to act weirdly around me. She became very attentive and complimentary. She insisted that we played in an outdoor badminton competition together, while Sarah not to be outdone put our names down for a tennis tournament. This new interest in me did not go unnoticed by Sarah. The holiday was over all too soon.

Chapter 7
Complications of the Heart

As the weather was gorgeous for the rest of the summer holidays we hardly stayed in. My conversations with Sarah when we were alone suggested that she might like to take our relationship further. But my heart now had mixed feelings. Even though my short romance with Meg was over some time ago the chemistry is still there and certainly not unnoticed by Ella. She was quick to talk about it just before going to bed one evening. I reluctantly explained that I did enjoy Sarah's company very much but there is no chemistry there at the moment. With Meg, I feel it is always simmering under the surface. Ella has always given sound advice when my heart is involved and what she said once again made sense. Later in bed, I made up my mind that I was in no particular hurry for a serious romance despite knowing that Sarah would be if I pushed it. I would see if my feelings towards her would grow.

That turned out to be a very bad decision. I had heard that my lack of hurrying had pushed Sarah into the arms of a colleague from school, who I know she had been seeing on a casual basis from time to time. My feelings for Sarah changed overnight. At least I had Alexa in my camp. For some reason, she hadn't taken to him and wanted Ella to ask me to try and win her back. Sarah and I were still jogging partners and involved together with Spartans, but some of the warmth had gone from our casual conversation making it clear to me that I had my chance and lost it. With Ella, Rosie and Alexa pushing me to keep trying to get our romance back on track, I decided on one last throw of the dice.

The next time Sarah and I go jogging I would tell her exactly how I feel about the situation. We had almost completed our usual route when I finally decided to bring the subject up.

"I am rather sad that you feel you need to give up on us romantically and find romance with your school colleague."

"I'm not in a romantic relationship with him. Even if I wanted to be it wouldn't get very far off the ground as Alexa doesn't like him. We have been out together for a drink a couple of times, but you did know about that."

"But you have given up on us though, haven't you?" I replied.

"The holiday made it clear to me that there were three of us in our relationship and Meg seemed to win all of the votes and make me feel insecure."

"I'm sorry you feel that way. If I assured you that Meg is definitely not in the picture and you are the one I want to be with, would that make any difference to your decision?" We arrived back at the bungalow and I was none the wiser.

Chapter 8
The Boyfriend Stage

I thought the early growing-up stages of the girls was a learning curve. The 'Boyfriend' stage was a tougher test for me. Ella had been seeing a boy for nearly a year now. Certainly not a boy of my choice. I had hoped that the relationship would burn itself out in time. But one night Ella asked whether she should think about going on the pill, which sort of confirmed that it was getting fairly serious. Rosie was also now showing an interest in boys but not Zoe.

The next problem I encountered left me as annoyed as I have ever been during my parenting experience. Ella had called me into her bedroom after an evening bath.

"Ella, whatever is the matter?" I worriedly asked.

"Dad I think I've got an infection, a sexual infection." With that, she burst into tears.

"Why do you think that?" I asked, trying to be calm and supportive."

"I've checked my symptoms online, so I'm sure."

"Do not worry, I will make an appointment at a clinic for a test."

The test proved that Ella was right. Her boyfriend had been cheating. Although Ella never wanted to see him again.

He had to be warned that he was contagious and could infect other girls. He usually came around on a Saturday evening and I was waiting for him. I refused to let him come in and told him that he had infected Ella, he immediately put the blame on her saying that she must have cheated on him. I reminded him that he needs to act responsibly and inform other girls he might have slept with as it can have serious consequences on their health. I firmly told him that he was no longer welcome here as Ella has obviously finished with him and that I was so disappointed with him as the whole family had made him very welcome. I asked him to admit the truth otherwise I would be having a conversation with his parents. Reluctantly he admitted that he was to blame and not Ella. Ella had been standing behind the door and had heard everything, prompting her to rush into my arms sobbing.

That evening after saying goodnight to Ella she called me back into her room wanting to talk.

"Dad, can I really talk to you without you being embarrassed?"

"Ella, nothing you have to say to me would ever make me embarrassed, you are my daughter."

"Before you talk to me do I need my 'mum's' hat on?"

"Probably," came the reply. With that Ella burst into tears. I sat cuddling her for an age before she said she was ready to talk.

"Dad, I have been so stupid and I am so ashamed of myself and I'm sure you are ashamed of me as well. I only did it once but I didn't really want to do it. I wasn't ready but I loved him so much and I thought I would lose him if I didn't."

"It sounds as if you were pressured into doing it and that's not right. Why didn't you make him take precautions?"

"I did try but he wouldn't." I felt myself getting really angry listening to all this.

"You were very lucky not to become pregnant, and hopefully having your infection treated quickly won't affect your chances of having children in the future if you decide to have any. Your ex treated you so badly and had no respect for you."

Ella looked horrified to hear all this. After a pause. "I think it would be a good idea to go on the pill."

"Why Dad? I'm never going to put myself in that position again."

"You say that now but you will have other boyfriends in the future but please make him take precautions until the relationship has gone some distance." One hour later, I went to bed.

With her infection now cleared up, she was in a much more positive mood as we drove to college on her first morning. Although close enough to get home at weekends I and the twins still missed her so much.

Chapter 9
Two More Departures from Our Family Friendship Group

I was so pleased that Ella was out of the way when the news broke that Mia was pregnant with Ella's ex-boyfriend's baby. I didn't hear it from Meg but when she did finally speak to me about it I suggested that Mia be checked for a sexual infection. It turned out that she was also infected. She admitted that she had slept with Ella's ex-boyfriend at a party when Ella wasn't there. It changed everything. Mia was no longer a welcome visitor and would not be staying over on a Friday night. Because of that Meg had to stop going to the badminton club. I also decided to give it a rest for the time being. In loyalty to Ella, I informed Meg that I would be cancelling Mia's Spartan's registration so she will have to look for a new football club if she wants to carry on playing football after her abortion.

When I told Ella the news about Mia her best friend at the weekend she was so upset. But at the same time relieved that she wouldn't be coming to the bungalow ever again or playing for Spartans again. Meg phoned several times and even sent a letter, hoping that all this could be put behind us in time.

Apparently, Mia was so upset about the football and not being able to see us all socially ever again. Meg pleaded with me to change my mind as I was the nearest to being a step-dad to Mia. I pointed out that it is unlikely that anything will change as Ella will never forget what Mia did to her and my relationship with Mia would never be the same. Meg finished the call by saying so that's it then after all these years. In a relatively short space of time, my family has lost four members of our close friendship group, including two teenage girls who at one time were close to becoming my step-daughter.

The bungalow seemed strangely quiet during the week. Ella settled into college very quickly and made friends with Amelia who lived fairly close by. Her dad and I agreed to take turns in picking them up and dropping them back to college. Both Amelia and Ella tried out for the girl's college football team and were successful which helped to raise Ella's spirits.

Meg and Mia were now out of our lives forever or so we thought. The coming weekend's match against Oldfield was just another fixture as far as I was concerned. Until a phone call from Meg changed all that. Mia had joined Oldfield and had tried to get out of playing against Spartans, but her coach wasn't having any of that. Meg asked if I could find time to talk to her for a couple of minutes when I see her. Meg went on to say that Mia is so withdrawn and sad and misses my family so much. I explained that I missed her and Mia as well as one time they were going to be part of the family. But I felt I had to be supportive and loyal to Ella.

Sunday's match came around soon enough. I warned Ella that she would be playing against Mia but there was no question in her mind about not playing. In fact, she played brilliantly in a one-sided match, scoring two goals with Alexa scoring the other two. Poor Mia didn't have the best of games and was substituted towards the end of the game. At the end of the game, I could see Mia looking over and wondering whether to come over, so in the end, I went over to her. Instinctively we hugged each other with Mia silently sobbing. I found it to be very emotional for me too because one time she was very close to becoming my step-daughter. When Mia had composed herself she asked if I could forgive her for what had happened. I said I already had, but Ella will need more time. I asked her whether she had completely recovered from her abortion. She said she had but because she was so ashamed she couldn't stop herself from crying all the time. Mia had asked whether they could all be friends again. I didn't make any promises but said hopefully in time. I also had a short conversation with Meg, but Ella kept well away but made it clear to me that she was unhappy with me for hugging and talking at length to Mia.

Ella was ready for a heated discussion as soon as we arrived back.

"Dad, I cannot believe that you gave Mia a hug and spoke to her after all the problems she has caused."

"Ella, you need to show some compassion to Mia and in time I hope you will. Having an abortion at a very young age has totally destroyed her. She is so ashamed that she cannot stop crying. She craves your forgiveness. She made a big mistake but needs your friendship so badly to get through this. It could easily have been you needing an abortion. I've tried to make it as easy as I could for you so you don't need to see Mia at all. But we have all suffered losing two more from our friendship group."

"I'm sorry Dad I'm never going to forgive her or be friends with her ever again."

"I'm sorry you feel like that because everyone deserves a second chance." It was my turn to drive Ella and Amelia back to college, which gave me a rest from another argument with Ella.

Chapter 10
A Romance Back on Track

Although my clear-the-air conversation while jogging with Sarah did nothing to suggest we has a future together we did seem close again. Although nothing was said, I had a feeling that with Meg now out of our friendship group Sarah was far more relaxed. The girls seemed happy that Sarah and Alexa were spending much more time with us and staying over most weekends and were comfortable with Sarah and I sharing a bedroom when they did stay over. We were now thinking of making it permanent, with Sarah keeping her flat for the time being in case moving in didn't work very well. But it did work very well from day one, without any teething problems so we were now a family of six, with me being outnumbered by girls.

Sarah got on well with all the girls and always seemed relaxed and unphased by any problems presented to her. The girls were very comfortable talking to her about the girl's problems, which was very pleasing but I have to confess I felt left out at times. Sarah's flat had been on the market for a couple of months without any real interest, which was to work in Sarah's favour in the future. We both had been so preoccupied with day-to-day living that we hadn't had a chance to discuss two major issues that needed to be resolved quickly. I had been living in a 'fool's paradise' thinking we would live happily ever after. I had briefly mentioned marriage but Sarah was against it having seen some of her friend's marriages fail, ending up with a messy divorce. Sarah had also said that she might like a baby sometime in the future. I thought our family was more than complete and didn't want to extend our family. These talking points were never mentioned again so I thought we had agreed to disagree.

Alexa was our next priority. Sarah had finally decided to tell her that she wasn't Alexa's biological mother, her sister was. She understandably wanted to know who her father is. Not getting an answer she stayed in her room all evening crying. Sarah was too upset to talk to her and asked if I could check on her to see if she was OK. I found her laying face down on her bed. I sat beside her gently putting my hand on her shoulder. Alexa after a while looked up at me and said, "Did you know?"

"Yes I did know, your mum and I had told each other our previous history."

"Do I call her Mum or Sarah?"

"I think you should carry on calling her Mum. She has looked after you since birth."

"And my dad?"

"Your mum's sister never said who he was before she died."

"So I don't have anyone to give me away when I get married."

"Are you thinking of getting married yet?"

"No."

"I would very much like to have that honour if you would have me."

"Why would you want to do that? Because you don't really take that much interest in me. I feel at times like an outsider. You never show me any affection and treat me like a daughter. I never get a goodnight kiss or a hug."

"Oh Alexa, I thought I would be overstepping the mark or make you uncomfortable if I did."

"I don't feel very loved at the moment. I thought I would be meeting my dad someday, but that will never happen now." Hearing all that I beckoned Alexa to come and sit beside me for a big hug. We sat there for a while not saying a word then Alexa announced that she did feel safe and comfortable with me. I responded by telling her that we would never let anything bad happen to her. I kissed her on the forehead and then asked her to go and see her mum.

The months passed and everything seemed to be going well. Until arriving home from school one day to find that Sarah and Alexa had moved out and back to their flat. Keys and a brief note saying, "it's best this way as our dreams are different," was staring at me on the table. Sarah wouldn't answer my phone calls and didn't turn up at the next Spartan's match and neither did Alexa. Despite all my attempts, including a visit to their flat, Sarah refused to speak or see me. Until one Saturday morning, Alexa came over by a bike. When she saw me she burst into tears. I gave her a big hug before asking if it was still OK to do that.

"What have I done wrong Alexa to drive you and your mum away? Has mum decided that she likes her school teacher friend better, is that it?"

"No."

"Did Mum not like me hugging and kissing you?"

"No, that's not it." That brought on more tears, so I decided to make her a hot drink to calm her down and sat beside her cuddling her.

"I'm in such an awkward position and Mum would be very cross with me if she ever finds out that I've been here." Alexa then broke the silence by saying that she always feels safe when she is with me. She then moved away from me and said, "Please don't be cross but Mum is expecting your baby."

I was stunned into silence. "But your mum was on the pill."

"She said that it must have been non-effective when she was ill that time. Mum knows that you didn't want any more children so that is why we moved out."

"Oh, Alexa." I couldn't but be emotional and Alexa noticed a couple of tears. It was her turn to be a carer as she wiped them away.

"Are they tears of joy or sadness?" asked Alexa.

"They are tears of great joy and are you OK with the news?"

"Yes of course."

"Maybe Mum will marry me now, but I better not push it just yet."

"If you do I will officially be your step-daughter."

"Would that be good?" A big hug suggested it would.

I cycled back with Alexa wondering what Sarah would say, knowing that I know about the baby. When I saw her I didn't give her a chance to say anything, as I rushed up to her to give her a big hug.

"I didn't deliberately become pregnant."

"I know, Alexa told me and please don't be cross with her, I'm so pleased that she came to see me. Please move back I've missed you both so much and so have the girls."

"We need to sort a couple of things out first." I offered to make a cup of tea first, saying that all good decisions are made over a cup of tea. Saying I would and actually doing it was a big challenge as I wasn't familiar with their kitchen. Fortunately, Alexa came to my rescue. I asked Alexa to come and sit between us as we talked and whispered to Sarah to give her a cuddle. That prompted Alexa to hold my hand, which surprised Sarah.

"Have you two been talking?"

"Yes, we have also sorted a couple of things out."

"Good, about time too," came Sarah's response.

As I left I kissed Alexa on the forehead and said goodbye step-daughter elect. She laughingly replied by saying goodbye dad elect.

Chapter 11
And Baby Makes Seven

Sarah and Alexa eventually moved back having finally convinced Sarah that a new baby on the way was fantastic news. We knew we had to think about another bedroom. We did think about converting the conservatory, but in the end, decided to have a new one built. The pregnancy went very well and it was no surprise to me to find that we were expecting a girl. We decided to name her Estelle after Sarah's sister. When Estelle did arrive, there was no shortage of help, almost leading to a rota being set up. She was going to be spoilt that is for sure. Sarah although a natural with motherhood, thought she might miss school life, so it was agreed that she would go back on a part-time basis after her maternity leave.

The lead-up to Christmas was drama free. Both Alexa and Ella were much happier. Alexa now felt part of the family and Ella was enjoying her busy life at college. The weekends were always open houses. Ella's college friend Amelia was a regular visitor as were the twin's friends. Mia was a surprise visitor too, wanting desperately to patch things up with Ella. Meg had previously phoned to say that is what she was planning to do. Ella said afterwards that it will never work.

Every time she saw Mia she is reminded of how she betrayed her with her ex-boyfriend.

Christmas was very quiet but magical with seven of us not budging from the bungalow. Sitting round the table on Boxing Day having just finished lunch. Sarah suddenly announced that we should have a New Year's Eve party. That stunned me as I thought that Sarah was not really a party person. Her suggestion was immediately backed up by the girls, so a party it is.

"What numbers are we talking, ten or twelve?" I nervously enquired.

"Don't worry about numbers, the girls and I will sort it all out, including all the planning and arrangements." The bungalow was now big with six bedrooms but the entertainment area was tiny.

I was beginning to be concerned about the cost when I opened the door to two delivery men. "Where do you want it?" one of the men enquired.

"Where do I want what?"

"The marquee." Sarah then came to the door and took charge of the situation. In bed that night I did ask how big is this party going to be, remembering how much money we had spent on the new bedroom. She put her fingers on my lips, whispered it's not your concern, kissed me good night and turned over and went to sleep. So that was the end of the conversation.

It seemed that every time I came into a room I found Sarah and the girls deep in conversation, but every time they saw me it went quiet. It was all getting too much for me. "Please let me be part of all the planning."

"No," came a chorus from the girls. Rosie pointed out that it is their project and they don't interfere when I plan holidays without their involvement.

I checked our joint bank account as you do from time to time, but I couldn't see any massive outgoings, which puzzled me. I was now getting used to opening the door to all sorts of delivery men bringing heaters, chairs, lighting equipment, and drinks, it was never-ending. The girls did ask me to set up the music system. I got another big 'no' when I thought I was now part of the team. I just cannot believe that I received an invitation through the post to my own party, but I did. New Year's Eve came soon enough and I haven't got a clue as to who has been invited. All the girls took ages to get ready and looked amazing, although a tad formal I thought.

"Dad, you should be getting ready soon."

"I am ready."

"You can't wear that, you need to put a shirt and tie on."

"Come on I will help you choose," said Ella.

When people started arriving I soon got into the party mood. All the Spartan girls were there with their parents, some of the badminton crowd, Sarah's and my friends, my sister and her husband and surprisingly Meg and Mia and Sue and Maisie. Everyone seemed to be getting on very well. I had a chance to speak to Ella. "Are you OK with Mia being here?"

"Yes, Dad, she will never be my bestie again but we are now talking." Having just toasted the new year in I certainly wasn't prepared for what happened next. All the girls went round refilling all the glasses again, saying that there is going to be another toast. With that Sarah appeared in front of me, went down on one knee and asked me to marry her. "Yes thousand times yes, but are you really sure?"

"Yes I'm sure," came Sarah's reply. Sarah had been planning this all along and everyone knew what was going to happen because they had a different invitation to me.

Alexa came up to me saying "does this mean" yes it does, you can drop 'elect' from step-daughter from your family title from now on." "Would it be alright if I called you dad from now on because you are a dad to me in every way?" "it would be my honour." A hug and a kiss sealed it. Curious Sarah wanted to know what that was all about. I just said that we had a couple of things to sort out. "And are they sorted?"

"Yes absolutely," I replied.

It was nice seeing Sue and Maisie. The party carried on until late, with only very few people leaving. We insisted that Sue and Maisie stayed over sleeping on make-shift beds and Ella's friend Amelia, who had asked me earlier if she could play for Spartans. Our sleep-over visitors stayed well into the afternoon, which gave me the perfect opportunity to have a long chat with Maisie before they left. She seemed a changed girl.

The girls were in bed very early that night. But Sarah and I stayed up fairly late talking about the party. I was intrigued by the fact that our joint bank account had been untouched by all the party spends. Sarah answered that by saying that the money had come through for the sale of her flat.

Chapter 12
The Honeymoon Period Is Soon Over

On one of our regular Saturday morning shopping trips, we bumped into Meg and Mia. We briefly exchanged pleasantries before going our separate ways. I thought afterwards how sad that it has come to this. In the past, we would have always gone for a drink and a snack. Although Ella didn't say one word to Mia, she did notice how much weight she had lost since the News Year's Eve Party. We didn't think too much about it until we saw Mia again. Meg had phoned asking if Mia could come round for some help with her homework as she was getting upset not understanding it. Meg dropped her off by car which was unusual as she normally cycled round. I was so shocked to see how much weight she had lost. She clearly had tried to hide it by wearing loose-fitting clothes. Meg had asked if I would drop her back home when we had finished.

The drive back was uncomfortable. Usually, when I'm alone with her she dominates the conversation, but not today. I decided to drive to the entrance of the local park and stop the car. "Why have we stopped here?" "Because we need to talk." After a lengthy silence, I opened the conversation.

"What's going on Mia?"

"Nothing."

"You have changed from being a very fit and healthy young girl to someone that has no energy, is looking very tired and has lost a great deal of weight. I am very worried about you."

Mia started to cry which is something I have rarely seen. I was about to give her a hug when she pushed me away saying, "I don't want you hugging me when you don't really care about me and I certainly don't want your pity."

"Oh, Mia, where is all this coming from?" With that, she shrugged her shoulder and sat in silence.

"Can I ask whether you are eating, only you used to have a very healthy appetite?"

"Yes, you can ask mum."

"Can we go now?"

"Yes of course," I replied. Not another word was spoken, not even a 'goodbye' as she got out of the car.

Later I phoned Meg, who assured me that Mia was eating everything put in front of her. I was also told that she flatly refuses to see a doctor about her weight loss. She has now given up playing football and going to her dancing classes. A couple of days later I received a very long, hurtful and sad text from Mia, which gave me some understanding as to how she was thinking and whether the weight loss was a deliberate action on her part to punish herself. She mentioned that she thought that her Mum and I would eventually get married and she would become my stepdaughter. She would never get over me marrying Sarah, as I had ruined her dream. She followed that by stating that she was so upset when I cancelled her football registration with Spartans and for stopping her from sleeping over on a Friday night when her Mum and I went to the badminton club. Her text also highlighted the fact that through making one mistake she has lost so much that was important to her. She went on to list that no decent boy would now be interested in her due to her past reputation, she is no longer part of a family that she loved so much and none of her good friends are very close to her now. Perhaps you can tell me what have I got left to look forward to?

It didn't take me long for the alarm bells to start ringing, having read Mia's text. I remembered something similar with a Year 6 schoolgirl a couple of years ago. She gave the impression she was eating normally, but she was forcing herself to vomit after each meal and was eventually hospitalised with anorexia. I phoned Meg straight away to voice my concerns and to read Mia's text to her. Meg said she would talk to her and that was the last I heard of it for a while.

I now had a problem that was surfacing close to home. Ella the girls 'shop steward' was beginning to show resentment of having Sarah as a step-mum and was encouraging Rosie to have the same thoughts. It was causing an atmosphere around the bungalow and was very upsetting for Sarah being told that she isn't their mum and can't tell them what to do. It was now beginning to threaten my marriage. When Sarah and I had a long talk about it I pointed out that Ella says exactly the same to me about not being her dad, from time to time.

It all came to a head when I was comforting Sarah who had been crying due to more cruel remarks made to her. Rosie was the first in the room and promptly burst into tears seeing

Sarah so upset and so did Alexa. Hearing all this sobbing brought Ella into the room. She didn't burst into tears but she at least gave Sarah a hug. After calling Zoe a couple of times she reluctantly came in but couldn't see what all the fuss was about.

After everyone had calmed down I felt the need to say a few strong words. "Right this needs to be said and I want everyone to listen carefully, please. Some of the cruel and nasty things that are being said to Sarah and myself from time to time are slowly tearing this family apart. Is that really what you want to happen? You girls don't know how lucky you are. You have a very nice home, you don't want for anything and you have a very caring step-mum and step-dad who give you large doses of unconditional love. Unfortunately, it is a bit one-sided at the moment. Now I know it is all a new experience having a step-mum but it is for Sarah as well. We are so lucky that Sarah agreed to take me on, she was also happy to take on a ready-made family of girls." With that, all the girls took turns hugging Sarah and me and apologising for the trouble they had caused. Estelle then wandered in and demanded hugs all around as well. We were all very hungry after that so a trip to Pizza Hut seemed a good idea all around.

I was now keeping in regular contact with Meg for updates on Mia's weight. Apparently, she was becoming a recluse, hardly leaving her bedroom and hadn't been to school for ages. She was now not eating, which was a major concern to Meg. A doctor had visited Mia and was in the process of arranging a hospital visit to see an Eating Disorder Specialist. I asked whether I could visit Mia, but Meg had strict orders to keep me away.

Over the months that followed the news updates on Mia worsened. She was now hospitalised, but not responding to treatment. Not helped by the fact she had all but given up. The concern was that if she kept losing weight her vital organs would eventually fail. I suggested to Meg that Ella and myself would pay her a surprise visit. So that is what we did. The shock of seeing the state of Mia was just too much for Ella who stood there speechless. She looked very embarrassed to see us, but as I moved closer to her she did manage a watery smile. "Oh, Mia please don't give up and fight this and start eating again. You have so much to live for."

A very weak voice replied, "Have I?"

"Yes, you have."

"I have lost everything I have ever loved and needed, you as a step-dad, Ella as a best friend and Spartans, for starters."

"We will always be close regardless and Spartans needs you back in the team. Your replacement isn't a Mia." I sat there for ages with my arm around her shoulders.

I could see that she was getting tired, so I got up saying, "Please try to get better for yourself and your mum, she is so worried about you."

"And what about you?"

"Yes, we need you and your mum back in our family friendship group where you belong." Ella then went up to her and hugged her. Mia quietly asked whether she was forgiven.

"Yes of course," was Ella's reply. Sadly that was the very last time that we saw her. Meg was in no fit state to organise a funeral, so Sarah and I helped as much as we could.

Chapter 13
The Older Years Through the Camera

Looking through the family photo album which I tend to do fairly often when I have an odd moment. I couldn't help but think that the life cards being dealt to me now have changed for the very much better. Family life is very good, long may it last. Whatever was happening in the family circle I was there with my camera. The older girls found this very annoying at times, but not Estelle. She was different. She was able to pose without any prompting and would be cross with me if she wasn't in every photo.

Looking back at Estelle's Christening photos I was reminded that she had been very difficult to please on the day and was grizzly, but she had been teething and not sleeping. She had been completely different at our wedding. We had deliberately delayed the big day until she was able to walk. That turned out to be a very good decision as she played the bridesmaid part brilliantly. She looked like a little angel alongside the other four bridesmaids. She completely took ownership of the wedding reception, wanting to show everyone her new shoes and doing endless twirls on the dance floor. We were all pleased with the wedding photos. Sarah and the girls looked stunning in all of them. Ella's new boyfriend Tom came to the reception. I couldn't help thinking that they looked so happy together and in love. Although Ella had previously decided on a lengthy period of boys are off limits and was taking their relationship slowly. I liked Tom he seemed a decent boy and was clearly good for Ella and both Sarah and myself had hoped something would come of it. Both Alexa and Rosie had the odd casual boyfriend but didn't come to anything. I did smile at the honeymoon photos. Anyone looking at them would have thought it was a normal family holiday. We had booked ten days in Spain but couldn't resist the girl's plea to come with us.

Zoe had finally admitted something that I had been waiting to hear for some time. She had never shown any interest in boys, but girls yes. I did feel hurt when she confided in Ella rather than discuss it with Sarah and me. But Ella had said that she must talk to us and eventually she did. I would not let her apologise for being who she is and all the family accepted it without question. We knew she had a girlfriend, but it was ages before we finally met her.

All the girls were now working. Ella and Zoe had excellent jobs. While Alexa and Rosie hadn't found the right job for them yet. Sarah was now back at her school full time with Estelle at my school in a Reception class. The photo of Estelle dressed as an angel reminded me of her class Nativity play. I had been sitting on the side of the hall with my year six class when the Reception class walked by on their way to the stage. A little tap on my knee as she walked passed to let me know that she had seen me and on the way back stopped for a hug and to ask me whether she had been a good angel. I thought that was so uncanny because Ella had said and done exactly that as an angel at her Reception Nativity play all those years ago.

Looking at the photos of all the different Spartans teams from the very first under fourteen girls' team to the present day. I was thinking about how things have changed. Most of the girls had grown up with the team, the difference now is that instead of parents watching and supporting the girls, it's now boyfriends.

Seeing a smiling and happy Mia in the photos reminded me of what a tragedy it was to lose her. Thinking back I was always consumed with guilt, even to this day. Although my loyalty had to be with Ella. I could and should have done more to prevent her from giving up on life. Sadly she felt she had no one on her side to give her the support she desperately needed. I'm always preaching second chances at school. But did I really give her a second chance when I took away her love from Spartans and her part in our family life? I will argue with myself forever over that. I did think a lot of that girl, we were very close, especially when her mum was seriously ill in hospital and it was touch and go for a while.

Both Sarah and I were very comfortable with the older girls still living at home and weren't looking forward to them leaving, knowing that it will happen someday. We were delighted that the girls still enjoyed coming on holiday with us. Although paying for them might have something to do with it.

A couple of my friends were staggered to find that I had six members of the opposite sex in my family, but I wouldn't have it any other way.

I did finally shut the photo album thinking that although it had been a struggle at times understanding the needs of babies to grown girls. It had all been well worth it in the end.

THE END